Puppy Club

DASH TAKES OFF

Catherine Jacob   Rachael Saunders

LITTLE TIGER

LONDON

Chapter 1

"And the winner of this year's *Britain's Best Baker* is…"

Arlo stroked Dash's curly blonde head, his puppy fast asleep on his lap, his eyes glued to the TV. The whole family – Dad, step-mum Sue and step-sister Sophie – had gathered to watch the final of his favourite TV show.

"I bet it's Alexander," Sophie piped

up. "His solar system showstopper was amazing!"

Arlo shook his head. "I reckon it'll be Cathy's lemon drizzle waterfall!"

"...Cathy!" the presenter announced.

"Told you!" cried Arlo, waking Dash, who leaped off his lap and began racing round the room, barking excitedly.

"I'd love to be on *Britain's Best Baker!*" said Arlo. "Imagine spending weeks on end baking delicious treats!"

Sophie licked her lips. "And eating them!"

"You'd both ace that bit!" Sue laughed.

"Hey, Dash! Calm down!" cried Dad, as the puppy zoomed past the coffee table, his tail flicking

6

dangerously close to a mug of tea. "I think it's time for a walk. This puppy has far too much energy!"

Arlo stood up. "Dash! Walkies!" As usual, Dash ignored him.

Dad shook his head. "Dash is nearly five months old. He needs to start coming when called or we'll never be able to let him off the lead."

Arlo felt a niggle of worry – Dad was right. He tried again. "Dash! Come!"

But Dash darted behind the sofa, thinking it was some great game.

"Dash!" cried Arlo. "How are we going to do a puppy training class if you won't even come?"

Dash and his five brothers and sisters were booked in for their first training session on Tuesday. The Puppy Clubbers had been looking forward to it for weeks but the nearer it got the more nervous Arlo felt – how would Dash cope?

"You go that end, I'll go this," said Dad, moving towards the sofa. Dash watched them, tail wagging. Just as Arlo reached out a hand, he dived through Dad's legs and bounded out of the room.

"Come back!" Arlo yelled, chasing Dash into the kitchen and round the island, until finally, with a little help from Dad, he caught him. Arlo fastened on Dash's new harness, which was meant to stop him pulling, and tightened the Velcro strap. Then he clipped on his lead. Immediately, Dash began straining towards the front door.

"Wait! Heel!" Arlo called hopelessly. Once they were outside, Dash woofed with joy, leaping up at Arlo before tugging him towards the street.

8

Dad watched as Dash pulled on his harness. "Do you want me to take him?"

"I'm OK," Arlo called, double looping the lead over his hand, just in case. "Dash! Heel!" he said firmly. The puppy ignored him. Arlo gritted his teeth. "Stop pulling," he pleaded, but Dash continued to veer this way and that, zigzagging across the pavement and getting dangerously close to the road.

"Those puppy training classes can't come soon enough," said Dad, as Dash pulled Arlo up a garden path. "If he doesn't— Oh! Hello, Daniel!"

Arlo looked up to see his best friend Daniel coming round the corner with his mum. Teddy, Dash's brother, was trotting calmly beside them. Calmly that is, until he spotted Dash!

The moment they saw each other the

puppies began yapping excitedly, crouching down opposite each other in a play bow, before leaping forwards, overjoyed to be reunited. As they tumbled over one another, Daniel's mum tried to untangle their leads. "Brotherly love, eh?"

Daniel grinned. "How's it going?"

Arlo shook his head as Dash's lead twirled around Teddy's. "He's pulling worse than ever this evening."

"You're lucky Teddy's so good," Dad told Daniel's mum.

"Teddy's no angel either," she replied. "He's really greedy!"

Daniel nodded. "We have to stop him from eating scraps off the pavement!"

Arlo and Dad laughed.

"We're hoping to get some help with Dash's pulling at the class on Tuesday," said Dad. "If he's tugging Arlo's arm off now, imagine what he'll be like in a few months when he's bigger!"

"I bet Dash will be a quick learner," Daniel said reassuringly.

Arlo sighed. "I'm not sure about—"

His words were drowned out by a motorbike whizzing by, its engine growling noisily. Both puppies let out a startled yap and raced for the safety of Arlo and Daniel's legs.

Arlo bent down and picked up a trembling Dash.

"Don't worry. I'm here," he whispered, stroking Dash's head.

Dash licked Arlo's nose as if to say "Phew!" then wriggled down and began pulling him away, up the street.

"Here we go again." Dad strode after them. "Roll on Tuesday!"

"See you at Underdogs tomorrow!" Daniel called after Arlo.

As they neared home, Dash finally seemed to calm down and Arlo allowed himself to relax. But as they turned the corner into their road, a cat suddenly darted across the pavement in front of them.

"Whoa!" Arlo cried, jerking forwards as Dash took off after it.

Dad moved in and grabbed the lead, holding Dash back as the cat flew under a bush.

"Watch out," cried Arlo. "Dash is slipping his harness! Don't let him escape!"

Dad bent down to check the strap. "It must have come loose with all the pulling. We need to keep an eye on that."

Once the straps were tight, Arlo took the lead again but the sense of calm had vanished. One of the things he'd been looking forward to most about getting a puppy was taking him for walks, but at the moment, they were just so stressful.

Back inside, Arlo took Dash through to the kitchen and took off his harness. The puppy barked happily and lay down on his back. Arlo laughed. "Oh! So you want a tummy rub now, do you?"

"Woof!" Dash replied.

Arlo sat beside him, any worries melting away as he stroked Dash's furry tummy. "I chose you because you're so full of beans! But when we're out walking, can you please try to be a bit calmer?"

Dash stared up at him with his big brown eyes, as if trying to understand.

Arlo smiled. "Don't worry, I'm sure the training sessions will help. And soon you'll be walking to heel, the same as your brothers and sisters." After all, training couldn't be that hard, could it?

Chapter 2

"Hey, Arlo, did you watch the final of *Britain's Best Baker* last night?" asked Elsa.

Arlo grinned. "Of course!"

"You should go on it," said Daniel.

"I wish!" Arlo replied. "Weeks of endless baking ... and tasting!"

It was Saturday morning and the Puppy Clubbers were counting out the lunch bowls in the storeroom at

Underdogs, the rescue centre run by Jaya's auntie Ashani.

The door opened and Joe, one of the volunteers, appeared carrying a tool kit.

"What's that for?" asked Willow.

"I'm doing some repairs to the kennels. Fixing the hinges and making sure they're secure."

Elsa's eyes widened. "That sounds serious."

Joe nodded as Ashani backed into the room, lugging a sack of dog food behind her. "Hi, guys! How are the repairs going, Joe?"

"To be honest," said Joe, "a lot of the kennels could do with a full refurb!"

Ashani nodded. "I know. But for now, I'm afraid we'll have to make do and mend – we just don't have the money."

"Are you OK, Auntie?" Jaya asked, noticing her aunt didn't seem her usual cheery self.

Ashani heaved the sack on to the counter. "I'm fine. It's just I'm going to have to turn another dog away as we don't have the room. A gorgeous dachshund. His owner will have to take him to a centre over an hour's drive away.

18

It's heartbreaking."

Arlo stared at Ashani. He'd never seen her look so upset.

"If only you could renovate that spare outbuilding," said Joe. "It would house another ten dogs, I reckon."

Ashani rubbed her eyes wearily. "We can't even afford to renovate the old kennels, let alone refurbish a whole new building! I've applied for some funding from the council but we won't hear about it for months." She gave them a tired smile. "Anyway, that's for me to worry about, not you. Now, Puppy Clubbers, how are you getting on with the lunch bowls?"

"Just finished," said Elsa. "Can we say hello to the dachshund?"

Everyone looked hopefully at Ashani who hesitated then smiled. "OK, just a quick one. His name's Bingo."

19

They followed Ashani to Reception, where Bingo was waiting on his lead, next to his owner. The little black-and-ginger sausage dog snuffled his nose into Harper's hand when she bent down to pat him. "Hello! Aren't you cute!"

The owner smiled. "I wish I could keep him, but we're moving abroad."

"That's such a shame," said Harper. "He's gorgeous!"

Arlo stroked Bingo's head. "I'm sure you'll get a lovely new home in no time, Bingo."

After they'd all made a fuss of him, it was time to deliver the lunch bowls, but Arlo couldn't get Bingo or Ashani's forlorn face out of his head.

As usual on a Saturday, the friends had arranged to meet at Jaya's in the afternoon for their weekly Puppy Club meeting. Of course, the puppies came too but it took Arlo and Dad so long to walk Dash round, they arrived half an hour late.

"Is everything OK?" Jaya asked, once Arlo's dad had waved goodbye. "We were getting worried about you."

Arlo looked down at Dash. "Well … after stopping for three poops and tugging me here, there and everywhere, Dash decided it would be fun to pull me into a queue of people waiting at a bus stop. Then he wound his lead so tightly round the bus stop pole it took ages to untangle him!"

"You cheeky pup!" Jaya laughed, pushing Dash down as he jumped up at her. "Let's get you through to the garden so you can run around with the others."

As soon as Arlo let Dash off the lead, he hurtled towards his brothers and sisters, overjoyed to see them. Arlo joined his friends on the picnic rug outside Jaya's garden playhouse, aka Puppy Club HQ.

"It's too hot inside, so we decided to stay out here," Willow explained. She was Top Dog this month and was proudly

22

wearing her Top Dog badge pinned to her T-shirt.

Elsa, who was Arts and Crafts Supremo, had made each of them a new badge.

Daniel grinned up at Arlo. "You look a bit hot and bothered yourself."

"I am!" said Arlo. He gulped down the glass of orange juice Jaya handed him, before relaying the bus stop incident.

"No way!" Harper giggled. She was Scribbler and the club notebook sat open in her lap.

Arlo, who was Snack Supremo for the third month in a row, opened the tin of flapjacks he'd brought with him and handed them round. Teddy came racing over.

"No, Teddy!" Daniel cried, pushing him away. "I'm sure he's part bloodhound – he can smell food a mile off!"

Elsa laughed and helped herself to a flapjack. "Mmm, these are delicious, Arlo!"

"They are!" said Daniel. He was Fact Finder this month. "Oh, by the way, I was doing a bit of research and found an article on how to stop puppies pulling so much." He reached into his rucksack and handed it to Arlo. "There are loads of tips, like making sure you stop when you're out walking and your puppy tugs on the lead. Oh, and it says harnesses are better than collars and leads, so you're doing the right thing there."

"Thanks!" said Arlo. "I'll read it later."

"Our pups are so lucky, aren't they?" Elsa said, watching them play.

Jaya nodded, admiring her Picture Picker badge. "I feel so sorry for Bingo."

"And for Ashani too," Arlo said.

"Having to send him away."

"Fingers crossed she gets the funding," said Daniel. "Then she might be able to build some extra kennels."

Jaya shook her head. "I heard Ashani telling Mum it's unlikely – there are so many worthy causes." She stroked Bonnie, who'd wandered over to say hi along with Peanut and Minnie. Everyone was quiet for a moment.

Then Willow piped up. "Hey! How about *we* raise money for Underdogs?"

Elsa's blue eyes widened. "Great idea!"

"But how?" Harper asked, looking up from the notebook where she'd been doodling Dash running round a lamp post!

"How about a sponsored silence?" Daniel suggested.

"Or a nearly new sale?" said Jaya.

Arlo held up a flapjack. "Cake sale?"

Willow turned to Harper. "Are you getting these ideas?"

Harper flicked over a page in the notebook and began frantically scribbling a list.

Jaya's face lit up. "How about a dog walk?"

"Yes!" Daniel exclaimed. "Owners could pay a fee to enter."

Harper looked up from the notebook. "We could call it the Waggy Tails Walk."

Willow clapped her hands together. "Love it!"

"So will our pups!" Daniel grinned as Teddy flopped on to his knee. "So many dogs together!"

Arlo watched Dash still haring round the garden. If the other pups were going to be excited, how on earth would Dash cope? Suddenly the idea of a dog walk didn't seem quite so much fun.

"Where would we hold it?" Willow asked.

"Maybe the park?" Harper suggested.

"We could sell refreshments," Elsa added. "How about a cake stall?"

Daniel grinned at Arlo. "Snack Supremo, what do you think?"

"Yeah, good idea," said Arlo distractedly, still imagining the chaos Dash might cause.

Daniel shot him a questioning look. "You OK, Arlo?"

Arlo forced a grin. "Yep. I'm fine."

Harper scribbled away. "I'll need to organize this into a proper list of jobs and—"

"Hold on!" Jaya cried. "We'd better ask Ashani if she's OK with the idea first!"

Harper stopped writing. "Oh yeah!"

"She always comes to see Mum on a Monday after school," said Jaya. "How about we put it to her then?"

Willow nodded. "Assuming she says yes, as Top Dog, I say we hold it as soon as possible."

Arlo put down his flapjack. Suddenly, he didn't feel hungry any more. As if on cue, there was a flurry of excited yips and Dash appeared. He threw himself at Arlo, licked his cheek, then tore off again.

Elsa giggled. "He's such a whirlwind!"

Arlo frowned. "Let's just hope Tuesday's training class does him some good."

"I'm sure it will," said Harper.

"Ashani says Jan, the trainer, is amazing," Jaya added.

"Read that article too," Daniel said

encouragingly. "Dash will be walking to heel in no time!"

Arlo forced a smile, but inside he felt a knot of worry tighten in his stomach. He couldn't even walk his puppy down a quiet street without something going wrong. An organized dog walk could spell total disaster.

Chapter 3

On Sunday, Arlo was still worrying about the walk when Daniel and Teddy came over for a play date.

"Teddy! Come!" Daniel called as they practised recall in the garden.

Teddy obediently bounded over to Daniel, who rewarded him with a treat.

Arlo's mouth dropped open. "How do you get him to do that?"

"Practice!" Daniel laughed. "Also, Teddy's so greedy he'll do anything for a treat!"

"I've practised loads with Dash and it makes no difference," Arlo grumbled.

"It will eventually," said Daniel. "Do you want to try now?"

Arlo nodded and held up a treat. "Dash! Come!" he called. Dash, who was wrestling a deflated football, ignored him.

"Dash! Come!" Arlo tried again.

"He needs to know you've got treats!" Daniel said.

Arlo ran over to show Dash the treat, but the puppy saw him coming, assumed a game of chase was under way, and ran in the opposite direction.

"I give up!" Arlo sighed, as Dash sprinted off round the garden.

Daniel patted him on the back. "The training classes will sort Dash out, you'll see."

"Will they?" said Arlo. "I'm worried Dash is untrainable. And I'm worried about him at the walk, if it goes ahead. I'm just … worried!"

Daniel stared in surprise. "Why didn't you tell me?"

Arlo shrugged. "I didn't want to admit it. All the other pups are walking to heel. Why isn't Dash?"

Daniel frowned. "Maybe you could ask Ashani for some tips."

"Good idea," said Arlo. "And thanks for that article. I tried the stop-start thing on this morning's walk, but Dash didn't like the stopping bit!"

Daniel grinned. "All the puppies have different challenges. Just try not to worry."

Arlo nodded, feeling a little bit better. "OK. I'll try."

At school on Monday morning, Mr Priest announced they were going straight to the hall for a special assembly.

Mrs Handy, the head teacher, was waiting as they filed in. "Good morning and welcome," she said, once everyone was settled. "I expect you're wondering what this special assembly is about? I have some exciting news. How many of you have been watching *Britain's Best Baker?*"

Arlo's hand shot up, along with almost everyone else's.

The head teacher laughed. "Well, I'm delighted to tell you that we are going to have our own Best Baker competition here in school!"

Arlo gasped as the hall erupted into excited chatter. A chance to take part in his own Best Baker!

Once everyone was quiet again, Mrs Handy continued. "As you know, every summer, we hold a fun charity event. In the last few years we've had a sponsored silence, a sponsored skip and an art competition. This year, you'll be raising money for a good cause either by baking cakes or buying and eating them! Those who'd like to bake will work in pairs to create a showstopper. The theme is the animal kingdom! I'm sending an email to your parents with more details and there will be a sign-up sheet in the hall until Friday."

Daniel turned to Arlo. "Partners?"

Arlo grinned and nodded.

"It's five pounds to enter," Mrs Handy continued. "And following the judging, we'll be holding a huge cake sale!" A list appeared on the big screen behind her. "I've put together a shortlist of six

36

wonderful local charities. Over the next week, you'll have the chance to vote for your favourite and the money raised will be split between the two with the most votes."

Arlo glanced down the list. There was a local food bank, a community garden and a nearby residential home, plus a charity that provided musical instruments to kids in deprived areas and a youth club. And right at the bottom … Underdogs!

"Yes!" said Arlo, high-fiving Daniel. They turned to see the girls pointing excitedly at the screen.

"The competition will take place a week on Friday," said Mrs Handy. "So you haven't got long to perfect your bakes. The winners in each year will receive a voucher for Lulu's Bakery in town and the OVERALL winner, as voted for by Lulu, will spend an afternoon with her at the bakery, learning how to ice cakes!"

"This is the best news EVER!" said Arlo, as they filed out.

"It's your dream come true, Arlo," Willow laughed.

"And Underdogs is one of the shortlisted charities!" Elsa cried.

"Wait till Ashani hears." Jaya's dark eyes sparkled. "I really hope it wins the vote."

"So who's going to enter?" asked Harper. "Besides Arlo, of course!"

Arlo grinned.

"I'm going to be his partner, or rather sous chef!" said Daniel.

Willow laughed. "With Arlo in charge, you guys have a great chance of winning."

"I'm not a baking fan," Jaya said. "But

I'll happily pay to eat cake!"

Willow nodded. "Me too."

"I'd like to bake," said Harper. "How about you, Elsa?"

"Definitely. Partners?"

The girls grinned at Arlo and Daniel. "Bring it on!" Harper laughed.

When the Puppy Clubbers arrived at Jaya's after school, Ashani was already there … and it turned out Mrs Handy had called her that afternoon to let her know about Underdogs. So the children launched straight in with their own fundraising idea.

"A Waggy Tails Walk to raise money for repairs," Ashani repeated slowly. They were gathered around Jaya's kitchen table. Ashani's dog Lulu, mum to the six

puppies, was lying at her feet along with
Jaya's pup Bonnie, who was snuggled up
beside her. Ashani's face broke into
a smile. "What a brilliant idea!"

Jaya gave her auntie a hug. "I knew
you'd say yes!"

Elsa and Willow high-fived.

"We really want to do something to help," said Arlo, although he still felt nervous about the whole idea.

Ashani beamed. "Thank you, all of you. I'll help you organize it, of course." She took a sip of tea. "Have you thought about a location?"

"Maybe the park," said Harper.

"It's a good idea but I'm not sure the council would give permission." Ashani paused. "I wonder ... what about the fields and woodland behind Underdogs, where we take the dogs for exercise and training sometimes."

"Sounds perfect," said Willow as Harper grabbed the club notebook out of her bag and started scribbling away.

"Derek, the farmer, lets us use it for free," Ashani explained. "Perhaps he'd agree to us holding the walk there too.

Leave it with me."

"Do we need to think about the distance?" Daniel asked.

"Good point," said Ashani. "Some dogs will be up for a long walk, but for others, like your puppies, twenty minutes is long enough."

"Maybe we can offer two routes – a longer and shorter one?" Elsa suggested.

"Great idea. We'll need a poster to help spread the word," said Ashani, her mind whirring. "I can put it on social media too and we can print off a smaller version to hand out as flyers."

"I can design the poster. I mean, if that's OK." Harper began to write again. "I'll add it to our To-Do list."

"You have a list already?" Ashani asked.

"In case you said yes," said Jaya.

Ashani grinned.

"We thought we could bake and sell cakes for extra money," Arlo piped up.

"Great!" said Ashani.

"How about you guys come to mine one night this week so we can plan properly. Maybe Friday?" Willow suggested.

The Puppy Clubbers all nodded in agreement.

"We'd better think about a date for the walk then, hadn't we?" Ashani said, reaching for her diary.

Please not too soon, thought Arlo.

"So … if Derek agrees, how about … three weeks' time. Saturday afternoon?"

Arlo's stomach lurched. Three weeks! Dash would never be ready by then.

"Perfect!" cried Willow.

"And it won't clash with the competition the week before," said Jaya.

Ashani grinned. "Between Best Baker and the Waggy Tails Walk, you're going to have a busy three weeks!"

Everyone laughed. Except Arlo.

Daniel gave him a nudge. "Arlo, didn't you have something you wanted to ask Ashani about?"

"Er, no, I don't think so," Arlo replied.

Daniel gave him a quizzical look, which Arlo ignored. Everyone was so happy, it just didn't feel like the right moment to mention his Dash worries. But how would Dash ever be ready in just three weeks? Fingers crossed Jan the trainer was a miracle worker!

Chapter 4

"Tell him to heel!" Dad cried, as Dash pulled Arlo down the street.

"I'm trying!" Arlo called back. But it was no use. Dash lurched ahead the whole way, and by the time they arrived at the puppy training centre, Dad and Arlo were red-faced and stressed-out.

They headed through a side gate and round the back. Jaya, Daniel and Harper were already waiting beside a fenced-off, rectangular training area. Bonnie, Teddy and Minnie were sitting calmly next to them as the children chatted to Jan, who had a swishy ponytail and was wearing dungarees. Dad said a quick good luck to Arlo and joined the other parents who were sat a little way away under a shady tree.

"Hi!" Jan waved.

Before Arlo could answer, Dash raced over to say hello, barking loudly and pulling Arlo after him.

"Don't tell me." Jan laughed. "This must be Dash and you're Arlo."

"How did you know?" Arlo asked.

Jan grinned. "The others have been filling me in on your puppies' personalities. Bonnie's shy, Teddy loves his food, Minnie's always sleepy, Peanut's inquisitive, Coco is feisty and Dash is a bundle of energy!"

As if on cue, Dash leaped up at Jan, to say hello.

Arlo was surprised to see Jan turn her back on the puppy. Only when Dash got down did she turn and kneel to give him a pat. "Good boy! Well done for putting paws on the floor!" She looked up at Arlo. "I know he's just being friendly, but you don't want your pup jumping up. Best thing is to turn your back until he calms down. Only then, give him attention."

Arlo nodded. He knew Jan was right, but why did Dash have to draw attention to himself before the class had even started!

Just then, Willow and Elsa arrived with Peanut and Coco and the puppies descended into a round of excited yaps.

Jan stood up. "I have a feeling this is going to be a lively class!" She introduced herself again, then pointed to the fenced-off area. "As they're all still a bit excited, we'll let them off the lead in the training area for a few minutes."

Arlo hesitated, worried how Dash would behave.

Sure enough, as soon as his lead was unclipped, Dash raced off and began zooming around in circles. Soon, his brothers and sisters had visibly calmed down. Not Dash, though!

Jan laughed. "Dash by name, dash by nature!"

"It's zoomies time!" Arlo muttered. "He gets like this at teatime."

"Don't worry. This is a new place.

49

He's bound to be excited." Jan turned to face the group. "Right, if you can pop your puppies on the lead, we'll get started. First, let's try some recall."

Everyone called their puppy and, one by one, they trotted over. Only Dash was left zooming around, ignoring Arlo's instructions. Jan held out a treat and called Dash over but Dash just ran back and forth, wanting to play!

Arlo felt his cheeks redden as a few giggles came from the others.

"Right," Jan said calmly. "Everyone stand still and quiet so Dash can concentrate." She kneeled down in the middle of the training area and made a little clicking noise with her tongue. "Dash! Come!"

Dash stared at her. She held out a treat and repeated "Dash! Come!", then made the noise again, until eventually Dash padded over to sniff the treat. Jan clipped on his lead. "I can see we're going to have fun with you!"

She handed the lead to Arlo, whose cheeks were still burning.

"Don't worry," Daniel whispered. "He'll settle down."

"The key with recall is to minimize distractions," said Jan. "When we were still and quiet, Dash was able to concentrate on what I was asking him to do. Hopefully, once he realizes there's a treat and lots of praise in it for him if he comes back, he'll start to connect the two." She smiled at the Puppy Clubbers. "Now I'd like to see what your puppies are like on the lead. Let's take it in turns to walk the length of the rectangle and back."

Jaya and Bonnie went first, calmly walking up and down. Arlo watched, trying to ignore the fact Dash was straining hard on his lead.

"Fantastic, Jaya!" Jan called. "Who's next?"

"Me!" said Willow, rushing forwards. Nosy Peanut kept stopping and sniffing at everything but once they were on the move, he generally walked to heel.

"Not bad." Jan smiled.

Clearly desperate to be on the move himself, Dash began barking and pulling harder.

"I can see Dash is keen," said Jan. "Would you like to go next?"

"Yes, please," said Arlo.

From the start, Dash pulled ahead so hard that Arlo could barely keep up. In the end he was practically running.

"I'm not sure who was taking who for a walk there." Jan laughed. "Dash needs to know you're in charge, Arlo. I'll give you some tips once everyone has had a go."

Arlo felt his cheeks burning again. Why couldn't Dash just be calm like the others?

Daniel and Teddy went next, then Harper and Minnie. Thankfully, Dash stopped straining and sat quietly next to Arlo as his siblings took a turn. But when Arlo bent down to whisper some praise, he realized Dash was only quiet because he'd been chewing his lead. "No, Dash!" Arlo cried, pulling the lead away.

Dash looked up at him, as if to say, *What did I do wrong?*

Once they'd all had a turn, Jan asked them to walk up and down again, this time, all together. This was far too

exciting for Dash, who at once began pulling towards the others. First his lead became tangled up with Bonnie's, then Teddy's.

"Watch out!" Jaya cried as Dash pulled across the line, nearly tripping her up.

"Sorry!" said Arlo.

Jan came over and took Dash's lead. "If Dash is pulling, Arlo, try this." She set off walking in a straight line. "Every time he pulls, stop short like this, say 'Wait', then stand completely still. Only when he's stopped pulling, set off again."

Arlo headed off again, with Dash tearing ahead, but though he tried to stop, Dash continued to pull. It was the same on the way back.

"It'll take a lot of practice," Jan said. "But you'll get there."

Arlo wasn't so sure.

The puppies' reward for working so hard was a game of fetch. Arlo had high hopes for Dash as he loved playing this at home, but here he couldn't stand still long enough for Arlo to throw the ball. He flew around, stealing the other pups' balls, until eventually Jan coaxed him

back. Then, to Arlo's dismay, she asked him to clip on Dash's lead.

"Why don't you two take a break," she said. "Dash is still a bit overexcited."

Daniel shot Arlo a sympathetic glance, but as Arlo led Dash over to the fence, he felt miserable. When the half-hour session was finally up, it couldn't come soon enough.

"I hope you all enjoyed that," said Jan. "The puppies have done extremely well."

Jan looked over to where the parents were waiting. "It's great that you were able to watch the session as it's important the whole family uses consistent communication. Remember to practise what we did today, and I'll see you all next week!" She turned to Arlo. "Arlo, can I have a quick word with you and your dad?"

Arlo's stomach sank as Dad walked over.

"I'm sorry about Dash!" said Arlo. "It's my fault, not his. I need to practise my instructions."

"Don't apologize!" Jan said. "Dash will be fine, but he's definitely a bit more energetic than the others. Not all puppies from a litter are alike."

Dad patted Arlo on the back. "You did a great job, Arlo."

"Your dad's right. Don't be downhearted, Arlo. I can see you're a really committed owner," Jan continued. "However, I think Dash might benefit from a few one-to-one sessions, until he's calmer."

"Just Dash?" Arlo cried.

Jan nodded. "The fact Dash chews on his lead and races ahead so often tells

58

me he's finding it a little more difficult to cope with all his bundled-up energy. It's not bad behaviour. I just think teaching him in a calm, quiet environment would be a good idea, and then we can reintroduce him to the group."

Dad nodded. "That sounds sensible."

"But … the Waggy Tails Walk!" Arlo blurted out.

Jan looked puzzled. "What's that?"

"We're organizing a charity walk for Underdogs in three weeks' time. Do you think Dash and I will be able to take part?"

Jan glanced at Dad. "Let's see how the one-to-one sessions go. I have a slot on Sunday if you're free?"

"Great," said Dad.

Jan gave Arlo a reassuring smile. "Don't worry. Dash will get there."

Arlo nodded but inside he felt like crying. He followed Dad through the side gate and round to the front. Everyone was waiting for them with worried faces.

"Everything OK?" Daniel asked.

Arlo shook his head. "Jan wants Dash to have some one-to-one sessions, but I just want him to be with the others."

"Of course you do," Willow said kindly. "But it sounds like a good idea."

"You're not the ones with a tearaway puppy," Arlo blurted.

Daniel shoulder-nudged Arlo. "Hey. Come on. Remember why you fell in love with Dash in the first place?"

60

"Because he's always dashing about!" Elsa chipped in.

"Dash was always going to be the boisterous, fun one," said Harper. "He'll soon learn."

Jaya looked sheepish. "I'm sorry I snapped at you during the session, Arlo."

Arlo sighed. "It's OK. I'm just worried that if Dash can't learn quickly, I won't be able to bring him on the Waggy Tails Walk."

Daniel frowned. "I'm sure he'll be fine by then."

"I hope so." Arlo picked Dash up and nuzzled his nose into the wriggly puppy's head. "We can do this, Dash, can't we?"

"Woof!" barked Dash, making Arlo, and everyone else, giggle.

"We'll work hard and make a great team, Dash," Arlo told him, feeling better for his friends' kind words. "Me and you."

Chapter 5

As agreed, on Friday evening they all went to Willow's for a Waggy Tails Walk meeting. As soon as they got in the door, Willow pinned on her Top Dog badge and they got down to business.

"OK," Willow began, "so let's talk about the location and date first. Jaya, do you have an update from Ashani?"

Jaya nodded. "Derek has given us

permission to hold the walk on his land two weeks tomorrow!"

"Brilliant!" Willow stood up and checked her wall calendar. "That's the twenty-ninth of June."

Arlo's stomach churned. "I hope Dash will be ready by then," he said.

"How's the training going?" asked Elsa.

Arlo sighed. "Not great. Dad says it's one step forwards, two steps back. And Dash still won't come when I call him."

Daniel gave him a sympathetic smile. "Remember, stay positive."

Everyone smiled in agreement.

"The next thing is the poster. How's that coming on, Harper?" Willow asked.

Harper took a laptop out of her rucksack. "Mum let me bring this to show you what I've done so far. I'll just fill in the date."

Everyone waited then huddled round to look.

WAGGY TAILS WALK
Saturday 29th June at 2 p.m.
Underdogs Rescue Centre.
2km or 5km walk to raise money for
a new building at Underdogs.
£10 per dog.
Refreshments available to buy.
To sign up your pup please email:
Ashani@Underdogs.uk

"I love the border with all the dogs following each other!" said Jaya.

"The purple and yellow lettering's

really eye-catching too," Arlo added.

Willow nodded. "It looks so professional, Harper!"

Harper beamed. "Thanks, guys. I'll email it to Ashani this evening."

"Shall we go through the rest of the To-Do list," said Willow. "Do you want to read it out, Harper?"

Harper closed her laptop and opened the club notebook. "OK, so, Arlo, you're in charge of cakes and biscuits, yes?"

"Of course." The thought of baking cheered him up a little. "Sue and Sophie are going to help with the baking. We thought we'd keep it simple. Maybe some puppy cupcakes and iced biscuits."

"Perfect. We can all help with the icing," Willow said.

"Do you think we should sell doggie treats?" asked Daniel. "The walking will definitely make Teddy hungry!"

Harper giggled. "Great idea."

"I can ask Ashani to buy those from the wholesalers for us," said Jaya. "Talking of treats, what's Dash's absolute favourite?"

"Er, cocktail sausages," said Arlo. "But he only gets them on special occasions."

"Have you tried using them as a reward?" Jaya asked. "If he really loves the treat, he'll be more likely to do as you ask."

"Thanks, Jaya," said Arlo. "That's a great idea."

"Right, what's next?" Willow asked, nudging Harper.

Harper scanned the page. "I've got down Start and Finish signs. I'm happy to do those."

"I can help," said Willow. "I wonder if

66

we need cones to mark the route?"

Jaya nodded. "I'll check with Ashani. Also, she said Sarita, Tom and some of the other Underdogs volunteers will be positioned around the course, acting as marshals."

"Brilliant," said Willow. "We don't want anyone getting lost!"

"How about we make some bunting to mark the start and finish? I can sort some materials from my craft stash at home," Elsa suggested.

"Lovely idea!" said Jaya. "You can all come to mine on Monday after school to make it."

"We'll need a sign and price list for refreshments too," Arlo chipped in.

Daniel's hand shot up. "Me!"

"And a table and a float!"

"I'll sort that with Ashani," Jaya said.

67

"Hang on!" Harper shook out her hand. "I can't keep up! Here's what I've got so far..."

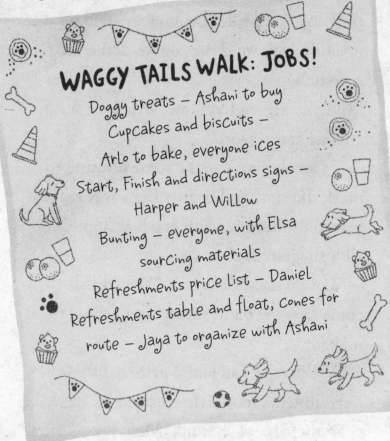

WAGGY TAILS WALK: JOBS!

Doggy treats – Ashani to buy
Cupcakes and biscuits –
Arlo to bake, everyone ices
Start, Finish and directions signs –
Harper and Willow
Bunting – everyone, with Elsa
sourcing materials
Refreshments price list – Daniel
Refreshments table and float, cones for
route – Jaya to organize with Ashani

"Perfect!" said Jaya.
A white ball of fluff leaped on to

Willow's knee. "Hey, Peanut! You're going to have the BEST time at the Waggy Tails Walk, aren't you!"

"They all will," said Elsa, then glanced at Arlo who was looking worried again. "A couple of sessions with Jan, and Dash will be more than ready."

"Fingers crossed," said Arlo.

"How about we have a walk in the park after Underdogs tomorrow, instead of our usual Puppy Club meeting, to give Dash a bit of practice," Daniel suggested.

"I'd love that," said Arlo. "But I'll have to ask Dad what—"

He was interrupted by the doorbell.

"Arlo, your dad and Dash are here!" Willow's mum called.

Arlo jumped up and ran to greet Dash, with his friends and Peanut hot on his heels.

Dad held tight to the lead as Dash began barking and jumping up, first at Arlo, then at Peanut, who was sprinting around the hallway, yapping a greeting too. "Someone's excited to see you!" Dad laughed.

"It's lovely to see you too, Dash!" Arlo told him, giving him a good scratch behind the ears. "Dad, are we free tomorrow afternoon?" he asked hopefully. "The others thought we might have a practice walk in the park."

Dad frowned. "We'll have to see. I'm not sure Dash is ready yet."

On the way home Dash pulled Arlo along as usual, though Arlo tried his best to follow Jan's instructions.

"We're stopping more than we start," Dad grumbled.

"I know, but hopefully the training will start to sink in soon," said Arlo. "Can we go to the park tomorrow? It'd be great practice."

Dad sighed. "I'm not making any promises, Arlo. Let me talk to Sue. Now, how was school today?"

Arlo smiled. "Daniel and I had a top-secret meeting in the library at lunchtime. We're going to make an Underdogs showstopper, with loads of little rescue dogs!"

Dad grinned. "Impressive."

"We're doing three tiers of sponge – chocolate, vanilla and lemon – then two different flavours of buttercream inside. One of the sponge layers is going to be Mum's special lemon drizzle recipe. I'd love to win it, to make you proud. And Mum too."

Dad stopped for a moment and pulled Arlo into a hug. "I'm proud of you every day, Arlo, particularly the way you're persevering with Dash. And Mum would be too." He smiled sadly. "She used to bake with you all the time when you were little. Whether you win or not, I know you'll try your best. That's the most important thing."

Chapter 6

When Arlo hurried into Underdogs
the next morning, the others were
already there, gathered around Ashani's
computer.

"Morning, Arlo!" Ashani called. "I was
just showing everyone Harper's poster
on our website. I only put it up last night
and twelve people are interested in the
walk already!"

Harper beamed. "Imagine how many we'll have by the twenty-ninth!"

Arlo tried to look excited, though in his head he was picturing Dash running wild among hundreds of dogs.

"Did your dad say yes?" Daniel asked. "To this afternoon's practice walk?"

"Yes!" said Arlo. "We had a real stop-start walk on the way here this morning, but Dad thought being in the park where it's quieter might be good for Dash's concentration."

Willow grinned. "Don't forget the special sausage treats!"

Ashani looked up. "Arlo, if you're worried about Dash, why don't you try to tire him out a bit beforehand? Play fetch in the garden for an hour or so before you leave. Really get him running around, so he's well-exercised already."

Arlo nodded. "Thanks, Ashani.

Nothing much seems to tire Dash out, but it's worth a try!"

Ashani smiled, then glanced at her watch. "Right, let's get going with those water bowls."

"Ready, Arlo?" asked Dad.

Arlo nodded, his tummy a jumble of nerves as he clipped Dash's lead to his harness. Dash stared up at him, eyes bright, tongue hanging out, tail wagging. The hour of fetch Arlo had just played with him in the garden didn't seem to have dented his energy levels at all! Arlo gave him a pat. Dash's tail started wagging even faster. "I hope you're going to use these lovely floppy ears for some good listening in the park!"

"Fingers crossed he heard you." Dad laughed. "Let's go."

The walk to the park took twice as long as it should have, although Dash did slow down a bit after each stop, which was an improvement. Eventually, they reached the big metal gates and spotted everyone waiting for them at the café near the tree-lined play area. Dash tugged Arlo down the path towards the other puppies.

It was quite a big group – as well as the Puppy Clubbers, Daniel's little sister and mum were there, along with Harper's dad, Elsa's mum, Jaya's dad and Willow's mum and her twin brothers. As usual, it was puppy chaos for the first few minutes. Arlo gripped Dash's lead as his puppy tumbled over his brothers and sisters.

"Everyone ready?" said Jaya, glancing a little warily at Dash who was chasing Bonnie around her legs.

"Yes!" they all cried.

The Puppy Clubbers led the way, with the others following behind. While the rest of the pups trotted calmly down the path, Dash pulled ahead. Twice Arlo had to stop and wait for Dash to come back to heel and by the third time, they had fallen a little way behind the group.

Arlo didn't mind too much, though.

In fact, he was delighted with Dash, who seemed to be walking to heel better now they were away from the puppy pack. Every now and then, Dad or Daniel would turn round to check on them and give Arlo a thumbs up. Arlo began to relax, and as they headed past a group of children from school, he waved proudly.

Suddenly, there was a loud whirring noise behind them. Dash stopped short and began to bark. Arlo spun round to see one of the park keepers driving up the grass verge towards them on a ride-on mower. As he came closer, the noise grew louder and so did Dash's barks. He began to pull towards the mower, barking furiously, but the park keeper had headphones on and didn't notice.

"It's all right, Dash, it's not going to hurt you," Arlo soothed. He bent down and tried to grab hold of Dash but the puppy was darting about too quickly to be caught.

Ahead, the others had turned to see what the noise was. Most of the puppies had begun to whimper and bark.

Arlo fumbled in his pocket for one of the sausage treats. "Here, Dash," he said, holding it out with a trembling hand, but Dash took no notice. He lurched towards the mower, then back again, clearly terrified.

Suddenly, Arlo heard Dad behind him.

"Just keep holding the lead, Arlo, and I'll get him," Dad shouted above the din. But as he reached out to grab the puppy's collar, Dash slipped out of his harness. The next moment he was streaking across the park heading for the trees.

"Dash! Come back!" cried Arlo, taking off after him.

"Dash!" Dad yelled, hot on Arlo's heels.

"Dash! Come back!" Arlo hollered

again, sprinting towards the wooded area after his terrified pup. He ran into the trees and stopped, but there was no sight or sound of Dash.

Dad caught up with him. "Did you see where he went?" he called.

"No!" Arlo panted. "Dash! Where are you?" His chest heaved in panic. He ran further into the trees, tears blurring his eyes. He heard a noise behind him and spun round. But it was only the others.

"He's disappeared!" said Dad, looking anxious. He put his arm round Arlo. "Don't worry, we'll find him. Let's split up and search the park. Someone must have seen him."

The adults quickly organized everyone into groups. "We'll retrace our steps to the play area in case he's run back there," said Jaya's dad.

"We'll head towards the back gate," said Willow's mum.

Daniel's mum ushered his little sister and Willow's brothers after her. "He must be here somewhere."

Harper's dad nodded. "There are railings all around the park so he can't have gone far."

"Let's head to the playing field," said Dad, setting off.

Arlo followed. They ran, calling Dash's name, asking passers-by if they'd seen him. One woman said she had seen a little dog with a trailing lead heading towards the playing field, but by the time they got there, there was no sign of him. A group of teenagers confirmed they'd seen Dash and tried to catch him when he ran through their game of cricket, but he'd been too fast and had headed down the long path that led towards the main gates.

After hearing that, Arlo sat down on the grass, inconsolable. "What if he's left the park," he sobbed. "This is my fault. I should have listened to you, Dad. We should never have come!"

"That's not true Arlo. Dash could have been spooked by a noise anywhere." Dad looked at his watch. "He's been gone fifteen minutes. Let's notify one of the park keepers – they'll help us look."

"What if I never see Dash again?" Arlo gulped.

Just then, Daniel, Willow and their mums hurried over. "No sightings, I'm afraid," Willow's mum reported.

Daniel kneeled down next to Arlo and put his arm round him. "Maybe the others have had more luck."

A minute later though they saw Jaya's dad's group running towards them. "Did you find him?" asked Jaya.

Arlo shook his head.

"Someone told us they saw a puppy with a red harness, but he was being led out of the play area by a woman and her son," Jaya's dad said, looking concerned.

At that, Arlo burst into tears again. "He's been dog-napped!"

"I'm sure he hasn't," Dad said. But his face was crumpled with worry. "OK, let's find one of the park keepers. I think we need to—" He was interrupted by the sound of his mobile phone. "Hello. Yes…" Dad's shoulders dropped as he let out a sigh of relief. He widened his eyes at Arlo, nodding frantically. "Oh, thank goodness for that! Please hang on a second while I let my son know."

"Has someone found him?" Arlo cried.

"Dash is safe," said Dad. "It's the vet. Dash was found wandering outside the park. A motorist who'd stopped at the traffic lights spotted him, picked him up and took him straight to the surgery! Thank goodness Dash is microchipped."

"He was near the road?" Arlo sobbed. "Poor Dash. He must have been terrified. And what if…"

"Don't think about what ifs, Arlo," Dad said, pulling him into a hug. "Dash is safe." He put the phone back to his ear. "We'll be right there."

Ten minutes later, Arlo and Dad were hurrying through the doors of the vet's. Miss Birchtree was sitting in Reception with Dash on her lap.

"Dash!" Arlo cried.

"Woof!" Dash barked, wriggling out of the vet's arms and running towards Arlo, who scooped him up.

"Thank goodness you're safe!" said Arlo, burying his face in Dash's soft fur.

Miss Birchtree smiled. "You stay here with Dash for a moment while I chat to your dad."

Arlo nodded. Dash began to nuzzle his nose into Arlo's pocket. "Aha! I know what you can smell!" Arlo reached for the bag of sausage treats and fed him a couple. Then the puppy cuddled in close to the crook of Arlo's elbow just like he'd done when he was tiny. "Don't worry. You're safe now," Arlo whispered.

For the next five minutes, Arlo sat cuddling Dash, who'd fallen asleep in his arms.

"Somebody's worn out," said Miss Birchtree, reappearing with Dad. "Poor thing has had an ordeal. Dogs hate loud noises – the mower must have been terrifying. A quiet afternoon with lots of cuddles for him, I think."

Once they'd said their thank yous, Arlo carried the still-sleeping Dash out to the car park.

"I've made a decision," he told Dad. "I've been worrying about whether Dash would be ready to take part in the Waggy Tails Walk but after what just happened, I don't think he should."

Dad squeezed Arlo's shoulder. "How about we see what tomorrow's one-to-one session brings and go from there. If anyone can get Dash ready for the Waggy Tails Walk, Jan will."

Arlo looked down at his sleeping puppy. What would he have done if Dash hadn't come home? He desperately wanted to do the walk, but keeping Dash safe was the most important thing. "Fine. But we're not taking part unless Jan is a hundred per cent certain he's ready."

Chapter 7

When they arrived at Jan's the next morning, Dash ran straight over, clearly delighted to see her again.

"Have you had a good week?" Jan asked.

"Not the best," said Arlo. He and Dad filled her in on what happened at the park.

"You know," Jan said, "I had a similar

thing happen with my dog Monty on a beach once. He ran off after getting spooked and we couldn't find him for an hour. The main thing is Dash is safe." She gave Arlo a concerned smile. "How have the walks been?"

"A bit better, but he's still pulling me along," Arlo admitted. "I stop every time, but it takes ages to get anywhere."

"Arlo's been following your instructions to the letter," Dad added.

Jan beamed. "Great. So let's start by letting Dash off the lead in the training area for a few minutes, to run off some energy."

At first, Dash sprinted around like he had during the group lesson, but without the distraction of the other puppies, he soon began to calm down. Jan entered the training area, kneeled on

90

one knee and held out a treat. "Dash!"
she called. "Come!"

Dash stopped and pricked up his ears.

"Dash! Come!" Jan repeated.

Dash ran over to her.

"Good boy, Dash!" She gave him the
treat, then clipped his lead on. "Come on
in," she called to Arlo. "Dash just needs
a bit of calm to learn what he has to do.
Your turn." She handed Arlo the lead.
"I want you to let him off, then after a
minute or so, call him to you exactly like
I did."

Arlo did as Jan said without much
hope of success. "Dash! Come!" he called.
To his surprise Dash stopped and looked
at him.

"Dash! Come!" Arlo repeated, grinning
in delight as Dash rushed towards him.
"Good boy!" Arlo exclaimed, giving him

the treat. "I can't believe it!"

Dad clapped him on the back. "You see! All your hard work is paying off!"

Jan laughed. "Dogs are like humans – they all learn in different ways, at different speeds. Now let's try some walking to heel."

Jan spent time showing Arlo how to vary the pace, to make it more interesting for Dash. "Walk a little, then trot," she called. "Walk again, then perhaps run a little. Keep talking to Dash all the time. And always have a stash of tasty treats in your pocket as rewards – *if* he isn't pulling. As soon as he starts to pull, stop short and say 'No!', then off you go again."

Arlo led Dash around the enclosure as Jan had shown him. It was great fun! After five minutes, Dash was doing brilliantly.

"Right," Jan said. "I think Dash
deserves a game of fetch as a reward."

Arlo nodded happily.

After the chaos of last time, this game
of fetch went perfectly. Jan had lots of
different balls, toys and ropes for Dash
to fetch and chew and Arlo almost forgot
they were at a training class.

"He's doing really well," Jan said, from the side of the training area. "But I think he's probably had enough now. You see how he's getting a bit distracted? Little and often is key. Call him in."

"Dash! Come!" Arlo's face lit up as Dash ran over to him. He gave him a treat. "Good boy, Dash! Brilliant!"

"See! He's really getting the hang of it!" Jan smiled. "Well done, both of you, that was a brilliant session."

Arlo clipped Dash's lead on. "Do you think it'd be OK for us to join in with everyone else on Tuesday?"

Jan paused for a moment. "If I'm honest, I think it would be good if we could have one more successful one-to-one session first."

Arlo couldn't hide his disappointment. Jan patted him on the shoulder. "But

if you keep practising what we're doing here, I think after another week, you and Dash may be ready to rejoin the group."

"I'll practise every day, I promise," Arlo said, determination surging through him. He reached down to stroke the top of Dash's head. After today's session, the Waggy Tails Walk didn't seem quite so impossible after all.

"Great news that Dash did so well, Arlo!" said Willow.

Jaya beamed. "I knew Jan would sort Dash out!"

It was Monday morning and the Puppy Clubbers were all gathered around Arlo in the playground before the start of school, eager for news.

"We're not ready to rejoin the group

class yet, though," said Arlo.

"Fingers crossed another one-to-one will do the trick," Elsa replied.

"Then you'll be back in the mix," Harper added.

"Remember," said Daniel, "Stay..."

"Positive!" Arlo shouted, grinning.

There was more good news in assembly. Mrs Handy announced the results of the Best Baker charity vote. "It was very close. But the two charities that received the most votes are … Banbury House Food Bank, and Underdogs Rescue Centre."

Everyone cheered, but Arlo and the rest of Puppy Club were extra loud!

"Wait till Ashani hears!" said Daniel, as they walked back to class.

"We'll see her later," Jaya said. "Remember, you're all coming to mine to make the bunting and she'll be there."

Willow nodded. "How's the baking going, guys? I can't wait to see your showstoppers on Friday!"

"Harper and I tried out our cake recipe last night! It was delicious!" Elsa replied.

Arlo spun round. "Oh yeah. What is it again?"

"Nice try," Harper said, narrowing her eyes.

"We haven't got time for a practice run," Arlo explained.

"We're just going to go for it!" Daniel grinned. "But I'm sure yours was really tasty. Chocolate, is it?"

Elsa rolled her eyes. "For the millionth time, we're not telling you!"

Daniel threw up his hands. "Oh, come on! You tell us yours and we'll tell you ours."

"Ha!" Elsa shook her head. "Not a chance."

Arlo laughed. "What goes on in the kitchen…"

"Stays in the kitchen," Harper finished.

Chapter 8

"Mum! Have you heard the news?" Jaya yelled, as they tumbled through her front door after her dad. "Have you spoken to Ashani?"

Jaya's mum appeared carrying baby Hari, with Bonnie running after them, barking a welcome. "Yes! She called me this morning to say Underdogs has been chosen as one of the school's Best Baker charities.

Isn't that exciting! She also told me fifty-five dogs are now signed up for the walk!"

Willow's jaw dropped. "Wow! And there's still almost two weeks to go."

"Fifty-five!" Jaya repeated.

"Sixty-two if you count our six pups and Lulu!" Daniel added.

"So that's a grand total of…" Elsa paused. She loved mental arithmetic. "Six hundred and twenty pounds!"

"You should all be very proud," said Jaya's mum. "And because of that I might just have a treat for you!"

Jaya sniffed the air. "What's that yummy smell?"

Arlo placed a finger on his chin. "I detect the unmistakable scent of chocolate chip cookies!"

Jaya's mum laughed. "You have a baker's nose, Arlo! Go through, everyone, and I'll

101

bring you the cookies and drinks."

Five minutes later they were all sitting in Puppy Club HQ, munching cookies and sipping on glasses of orange squash.

"I still can't get over how much money we've made already!" Daniel said.

Arlo nodded. "Over six hundred pounds is brilliant."

"I heard Ashani telling Mum the other day that she's getting costs to turn the outbuilding into ten new kennels," Jaya said knowledgably. "One quote was six thousand pounds!"

Willow whistled. They were all quiet for a moment as the figure sank in. "Well, we're making a great start on that," said Willow.

Elsa nodded. "True. I wouldn't be surprised if…" She paused, totting up the numbers in her head. "We get close to a thousand pounds!"

"A sixth of the way there!" Harper exclaimed.

Willow leaped up. "Right. Let's get cracking. Talking isn't going to make this bunting, is it?"

Ella pulled a bundle of coloured card out of her bag. "Mum showed me an easy way to make the triangles," she said, showing them how to fold a square of card diagonally, to make two pieces of bunting.

Soon, they were all busily cutting away and had a pile of triangles ready to string together.

"Fingers crossed it doesn't rain or this'll be very soggy bunting!" Daniel laughed.

"Don't worry," Elsa said. "I have sticky-back plastic to cover each triangle."

Willow grinned admiringly. "You've thought of everything!"

On Tuesday, Daniel came home with Arlo
to work on their showstopper. The Best
Baker competition was three days away
and they had lots to do! Daniel only had
an hour before his dad picked him up for
puppy training classes so they set to work
immediately on making decorations for the
cake out of coloured icing. When the hour
was up, they'd crafted Lulu, the six pups,
plus lots of extra dogs, some tiny water
bowls, leads, bones and balls too!

"I'm not sure this looks much like
Ashani!" said Daniel, holding up his
fondant figure.

Arlo grinned at his own creation of
chocolate sticks and marzipan. "This isn't
an exact replica of Underdogs either.
But we've done our best."

Sue strolled in. "Daniel, remember
your dad will be here in a minute to take
you to Jan's."

Daniel leaped off the kitchen stool.
"Thanks for the reminder. Are you OK
to finish up by yourself, Arlo?"

Arlo forced a smile. "Course. Have
fun!"

"It won't be as fun without you," said
Daniel.

"Don't worry, we'll be there next week," Arlo said, hoping he sounded more confident than he felt.

Once Daniel had gone, Arlo cleared up and left the cake toppers to harden. Dash bounded in from the garden so Arlo got down on the floor and grabbed a toy, holding it out for him to paw. "I wish we were going to puppy training too, Dash."

"Woof!" Dash replied.

"We'll just have to work extra hard to make sure we're there next week. And then…"

Arlo heard the front door open then shut. It was Sophie coming back from her friend Sabrina's, where they'd been working on their showstopper. He'd just managed to hide the cake toppers under a cake box when Sophie appeared. "Hey, Arlo." She peered at the box. "Ooh, what's under there? Can I have a look?"

Arlo shook his head. "Not a chance! How did your showstopper go?"

"Really well!" Sophie giggled. "Give or take a few cracked eggs on the floor! Where's Daniel?"

"Gone to puppy training class," Arlo mumbled.

"Ah."

Dash rolled over in front of her. "Oh, I know what you want!" Sophie kneeled down and gave Dash a tummy rub. She looked up at Arlo. "Are you OK?"

Arlo shrugged. "I'm just a bit sad we're not at training."

Sophie nodded. "Look on the positive side, you and Dash get your very own training session on Sunday. After which,

Dash will have caught up with the others."

Arlo smiled. "Hopefully!"

"How about we take him in the garden and try some recall now? What do you think, Dash?"

At the mention of his name, Dash scrambled to his feet.

"See! Dash is up for it," said Sophie.

Arlo grinned, suddenly feeling happier. "Thanks, Sophie. Let's go!"

Chapter 9

"You should have your own cookery show!" Daniel said, watching Arlo pour another batch of cake batter into a tin.

It was Thursday and the boys had gone back to Arlo's after school to bake and ice their showstopper. Sophie was at Sabrina's again so they had the kitchen to themselves.

"Zingy, but delicious!" Daniel

exclaimed as he tasted the lemon sponge mix.

"And how awesome does the chocolate one smell?" said Arlo.

"Amazing!" Daniel grinned.

Just then, the oven timer beeped, so under Sue's watchful eye, Arlo carefully checked the chocolate sponge was cooked, using a metal skewer. "Clean! I'd say it's done! Let's swap it for the lemon and vanilla sponges."

Once all the cakes were baked and cooling, they had tea.

"How did this morning's walk go?" Daniel asked, watching Dash play with a toy outside the kitchen window.

"OK, actually," Arlo replied. "Varying the pace seems to keep Dash on the ball and he loves the sprinting bit best of all! I only had to stop and wait about five times."

Daniel fist-bumped him. "You see! All your practice is working!"

Arlo grinned. "I have to admit, it is!"

Once they'd finished eating, it was time to put the showstopper together. Arlo showed Daniel how to cut round the sponges to loosen the edges from the tin. Then he took two bowls from the fridge. "I made the buttercream last night – chocolate and lemon. Let's start with the chocolate."

Carefully, they sandwiched the chocolate and lemon cakes together with a thick layer of buttercream. Then they smoothed the lemon buttercream on top of the lemon cake and added the vanilla sponge on top.

"I'm glad we didn't have pudding," Daniel giggled as they licked icing from the spoons. "This chocolate buttercream's awesome!"

Arlo gave his spoon a big lick. "Isn't it! Now we need to cover the whole thing in the green, ready-rolled icing. This is the trickiest bit."

He carefully removed the sheet of icing, then they took one side each. "Ready … lift!" They hovered it over the top of the cake, but just as they did so, the kitchen door banged open and Dash flew through. He bounded over to them, jumping up at Arlo's legs.

"Dash! No!" Arlo cried. As he moved to avoid Dash, the icing sheet tore in two and flopped on to the cake below!

"Uh-oh!" Daniel grimaced.

Arlo stared in dismay. "It's ruined!"

"I'm sure we can fix it," Daniel said reassuringly.

Arlo took a deep breath. Best Baker contestants didn't panic when things went wrong. "Dash! Come!" he said in a firm voice, wavering a little as Dash stared up at him innocently. "Don't give me those puppy-dog eyes!" Arlo said, leading him out of the door and shutting it firmly. "OK. Let's see what we can do." He peeled the sheet of icing off the cake. "We'll squish it together then roll it out again and see what happens. Hopefully it won't look too bad."

Arlo set to work, shaping the icing into a ball and then rolling it out. It was a bit bumpy and sticky in places, and it was far from the perfect showstopper

he'd had in his head, but it would have to do. Gingerly, they laid it over the cake and trimmed the edges. Arlo stood back. He sighed. Lumpy, but not too terrible! "There's not much more we can do, so let's just move on to the fun part – the cake toppers."

Twenty minutes later, their showstopper was finished.

"It looks awesome!" said Daniel.

Arlo smiled proudly. "I wonder how Elsa and Harper are getting on."

"Hope it's not an Underdogs cake too!" Daniel laughed.

The door opened and Dad and Sue walked in, a sheepish-looking Dash behind them.

Arlo gave him a reassuring pat. "It's OK, Dash. We sorted it."

"Wow!" said Dad. "That cake looks…"

115

"Epic?" Arlo grinned.

"Exactly!"

Arlo picked Dash up to show him. "Look! That's you on there, dashing around with the other dogs!"

"Woof!" Dash barked and licked Arlo's cheek.

Dad smiled. "You should both be super proud of yourselves."

On Friday morning, Arlo sprang out of bed – competition day! After a quick breakfast, they were soon in the car on the way to school. Arlo had the Underdogs showstopper in a huge cardboard box on his knee and Sophie spent the whole journey trying to persuade him to give her a sneaky peek. When they arrived at school, Arlo carefully carried the box over to Daniel who was already in the queue of children waiting to drop their cakes off in the hall.

"So many entries!" said Arlo.

Daniel nodded. "Mrs Handy's making sure each pair go in separately, so it's anonymous."

Five minutes later they reached the front. Inside the hall, Mrs Handy pointed to a long table covered in amazing showstoppers. "Morning, boys! Year Four's section is over there."

"Wow!" Arlo and Daniel chorused, as they walked past the Year Five and Six tables. There were all sorts of cakes, including a zoo, a shepherd with his flock

of sheep and a long, jewelled snake. Over on the Year Four table, Arlo spotted an Arctic scene with an igloo and polar bears and the most beautiful rainforest with monkeys, parrots and a crystal-blue river. Would they really be in with a chance against these?

Together, they carefully lifted their showstopper out and placed it on the table.

Daniel blew out his cheeks. "The competition's tough."

"Isn't it!" Arlo agreed.

Throughout the morning, each class visited the hall to vote. When it was Class Four's turn, Mr Priest handed them each a slip of paper and a pencil. "You have one vote for your favourite showstopper in Year Four. And remember, you can't vote for your own!"

Arlo looked over at Elsa and Harper, who were standing by the Underdogs cake, smiling and whispering. They'd obviously guessed it was Arlo and Daniel's. Arlo wandered up and down

120

the other creations. Which one was
Harper and Elsa's? There was a stunning
butterfly covered in jewel-coloured
sweets, an amazing farmyard scene and
twenty-four safari cupcakes – each one
made to look like a different animal!
However, Arlo kept coming back to the
rainforest cake. There was something so
beautiful about the sparkling river, he had
to vote for it.

After they'd handed in their judging
slips, they headed outside for breaktime.

"OK, which of you made Underdogs?"
Willow cried. "It was brilliant."

Arlo and Daniel pointed at one
another.

"I voted for it!" said Jaya.

"Me too!" Elsa smiled. "Not just
because I worked out it was yours.
I absolutely loved it."

Harper nodded. "And me!"

"I voted for the rainforest cake," Arlo said. "That was my favourite."

"Me too!" Daniel exclaimed.

It was the girls' turn to grin. "That was ours!"

"How did you make the river?" Arlo asked.

"Melted blue boiled sweets!" said Harper. "I saw one of the contestants do it last year on *Britain's Best Baker.*"

Elsa laughed. "It might look great but I don't think Lulu will be impressed by the taste!"

Harper nodded. "We burned the sponge and it's as hard as rock!"

"Well, it looks awesome!" Arlo said.

"So does yours!" said Elsa, holding up her hand for a group high five. "May the best showstopper win!"

Chapter 10

The school hall had floor-to-ceiling windows on the side next to the junior playground, so throughout the day, Arlo, along with the whole school, couldn't help taking sneaky peaks as chief judge Lulu wandered up and down the tables tasting the showstoppers. Whose cake would she pick?

Finally, with half an hour to go before

the end of school, Mrs Handy called
everyone into the hall. Lulu was standing
next to her, beaming. The sweet smell
of cakes swirled through the air. Nerves
swirled around Arlo's tummy. So this
is what *Britain's Best Baker* contestants
must feel like!

"Hello and welcome to the Best
Baker!" Mrs Handy paused. "I've always
wanted to say that!"

Everyone laughed.

"What an amazing array of cakes! Give
yourselves a clap!"

The hall erupted into applause and
cheers before Mrs Handy called for quiet.

"The winning cakes in each year are
behind this table! So, without further
ado, I'll hand over to our head judge,
Lulu of Lulu's Bakery."

Everyone clapped again as Lulu

stepped forwards, wearing an apron covered in rainbow cupcakes. She beamed around at everyone. "I have been baking for twenty-five years and I have never seen such an eclectic selection of cakes! You should be proud of yourselves. I'm going to announce the winners of each year as voted by all of you, then at the end, the overall winning showstopper as judged by me from the seven finalists! First, Reception's Best Baker winners are..."

The hall fell silent.

Lulu reached under the table and brought out a large pink elephant, with one slice cut out! "Suzy Barber and Anita Haq with their raspberry and almond Ellie Elephant showstopper!"

Everyone clapped as Suzy and Anita made their way up to shake Lulu's hand.

Lulu continued to reveal the winning showstoppers from Year One, Two and Three – a caramel and chocolate wolf cake, a mint choc chip penguin colony and a stunning pistachio bird-feeder cake decorated with real flowers! Finally, it was time for Year Four.

Daniel gripped Arlo's arm.

Arlo tried to ignore his nerves.

"The winner is..." Lulu reached under

the table. "Arlo and Daniel's chocolate, vanilla and lemon Underdogs Rescue Centre showstopper!"

As everyone clapped, Arlo's stomach did a little flip.

At the end of their row, Willow, Harper, Elsa and Jaya cheered and Sophie's loud whoops reached Arlo's ears from the Year Six bench.

Arlo followed Daniel up to shake hands with Lulu. "Can I just say that every single mouthful I tried was delicious, but that lemon sponge layer was sublime! Are you both keen bakers?"

Arlo opened his mouth but found himself lost for words!

Daniel pointed at Arlo. "He's the baker. I'm his sous chef."

Lulu winked at Arlo. "You need to give me the recipe for that lemon sponge!"

"It was my mum's recipe," Arlo said proudly.

As they walked back to their places holding their vouchers, Elsa, Jaya, Harper and Willow high-fived them as they passed.

Once the Year Five and Six winners were revealed, it was time for Lulu to announce the overall winner. "Now, imagine how difficult it was for me to choose from these seven amazing creations. I judged the cakes not only on how they look – and there were some really professional-looking cakes – but also on taste and texture. The overall

128

winner certainly looks stunning, and it tastes sublime. It is…"

A hush fell over the hall.

"Lucy and Oruj's pistachio Bird-Feeder showstopper!"

A thunderclap of applause rolled around the hall mingled with cheers and whoops. Arlo couldn't help sharing a little glance of disappointment with Daniel, but they both cheered loudly as the girls picked their way through the sea of children.

Once the cheers had died down, Lulu presented them with their prize. "I'd also like to give a special mention to one more cake. If I had been judging on taste alone, this would have been my winner. I have a cookery book as a consolation prize for … Arlo and Daniel and their Underdogs Rescue showstopper!"

Daniel pulled Arlo to his feet and pushed him towards the front. "You did it!"

"No, *we* did it!" Arlo shot back. "Together."

"Congratulations again!" Lulu told him. "I have no doubt, Arlo, if you keep baking like this, you'll have a bright future ahead of you! I look forward to buying your cakes one day."

Arlo beamed.

"You can buy some next Saturday!" Daniel blurted out. "At our Waggy Tails Walk in aid of Underdogs."

Lulu smiled. "Oh, really? Well, it just so happens I have a dog. I'd love to come along. As long as you promise to save me some cake!"

Mrs Handy stepped up beside them. "Talking of which, I hope you've all brought your money along, because it's now time for the cake sale!"

130

After the excitement of Best Baker, for
Arlo, the weekend was all about Dash.
The Waggy Tails Walk was now only a
week away. On Sunday, Jan would decide
if they could take part.

On Saturday afternoon, the Puppy
Clubbers brought their pups to
Underdogs to check out the route, with
Ashani and Lulu. After the accident with
the icing, Arlo couldn't help worrying
that Dash's excitable ways would cause a
problem on the walk, but it turned out
he had no need to worry. Dash behaved
perfectly and Arlo hardly had to stop at
all to pull him back.

Everyone was impressed.

"How many have signed up now,
Ashani?" Jaya asked as they skirted

around the edge of the field.

"A hundred and three! I've actually closed entries now, or it might get a little out of hand."

"So that's one thousand and thirty pounds in entry money alone!" said Elsa.

"And we should make at least a few hundred maybe from the refreshments," Arlo piped up.

"Don't forget the money raised from the Best Baker competition and cake sale," Harper added.

Willow nodded. "Mrs Handy said we made nearly four hundred pounds altogether."

"So Underdogs gets two hundred of that!" Daniel chipped in.

Ashani beamed. "We're already well over one sixth of the way towards the new wing and it's all thanks to you!"

On Sunday, the first half of the one-to-one lesson went even better than Arlo could have hoped for.

"You know," Jan said, "I think it's time to take Dash for a walk around the block."

Arlo frowned. "Are you sure?"

"Absolutely. Though of course out on the street, Dash is bound to feel more excited and less likely to do as he's asked."

Arlo nodded, suddenly nervous.

"Just remember," Jan said. "If he pulls, stop. Praise Dash once he's still. Then walk on."

They set off, Arlo following Jan's instructions to the letter. Dad looked on from a little way behind. Dash wasn't perfect, but he was definitely pulling far less than usual and most importantly, he responded to all of Arlo's instructions.

"How did that feel?" Jan asked once they were back in the training area.

"Good!" Arlo exclaimed.

Dad grinned. "He's like a different dog."

Jan nodded. "He's learning. That's all. Well done, Arlo. You've worked really hard."

"Thanks!" Arlo smiled proudly.

"So, would you like to rejoin the group class on Tuesday?" Jan asked.

Arlo gasped. "Yes, please!"

"Great. I'll see you then!"

"Thank you!" Arlo turned to lead Dash away, then he spun round. "Do you think Dash might be OK for the Waggy Tails Walk?" he asked.

Jan grinned. "I knew you'd ask that and the answer is, let's take a final call on

Tuesday but honestly, I think he'll be just fine."

On Tuesday at Jan's, everyone was excited to see Dash in action and to Arlo's relief, the class was a triumph!

"I can't believe it," Jaya said afterwards. "What a transformation!"

Daniel gave Dash a scratch behind his ears. "You were so good, Dash!"

"A different puppy from two weeks ago," Harper added.

"Yes," said Jan, coming over. "He's come on leaps and bounds!"

Arlo nodded. "So ... do you think we'll be OK for Saturday?"

Jan grinned. "Absolutely! Just remember not to panic if Dash suddenly gets overexcited. Stay calm and give clear instructions, rewarding him each time he does what you ask."

The rest of the week was a whirl of ingredient buying and baking. Arlo, Sophie and Sue had decided to bake twenty-four cookies and cakes every night and freeze them. Then on Friday evening, all six Puppy Clubbers gathered in Arlo's kitchen to ice them.

Arlo held up a cupcake to demonstrate. "First you swirl the chocolate buttercream on top, then you place a large chocolate button on each side like this!"

"Ears!" Willow cried in delight.

Arlo nodded. "Use two white choc chips for eyes, a dark choc chip for the nose, then finally, a pink jelly sweet for the tongue. And voilà! A puppy cupcake!"

"You mean a pupcake!" Jaya grinned.

For the next half an hour, they all had great fun creating their pupcakes, though unsurprisingly, not all the choc chips made it on to the cakes!

They were just having a break before icing the biscuits when Sue came into the kitchen clutching her mobile. "It's Ashani!" She put her on speaker.

"Hi, guys," said Ashani, sounding excited. "Guess what! I've had a call from the local paper. One of their reporters saw our poster on Twitter and thought it would make a great story, so they're coming to take photographs and want to interview me and all of you!"

"Yaaaaaay!" Willow squealed as the Puppy Clubbers leaned in for a high five.

"Underdogs will be famous!" Arlo cried.

Chapter 11

Saturday morning finally arrived. With a boot full of cookies and pup cakes, and Dash, clipped into his puppy seat belt, Arlo's dad drove the family to Underdogs. Once there, they went round to the field, which was already a hive of activity.

"The First Underdogs Waggy Tails Walk!" Ashani was reading from a banner, as Harper's mum and dad hung it across two trees. "Brilliant!"

Harper beamed.

Jaya, Willow, Daniel and Elsa were busy setting up a line of tables for the refreshments stall.

Daniel came running over. "Hi, Dash!" He bent down to pet the excited puppy.

"Where's Teddy?" Arlo asked.

Daniel pointed. "Ashani's made a little fenced-off area for the pups to run around in while we're busy."

"Cool. I'll pop Dash in with them," Arlo said.

"Morning, Arlo!" Ashani called. "Can I give you two a job once Dash is settled? These 'This Way' signs need to go up, to show people where to come when they arrive."

There was so much to do – putting up bunting, toilet signs, sorting the float, setting out refreshments and checking the cones for the route. They just had time to grab a sandwich for lunch before the reporter and photographer arrived. They chatted to Ashani for a few minutes then beckoned the Puppy Clubbers over.

"Hi, everyone," said the photographer. "What an amazing afternoon you've organized. We'd like to do a quick interview before taking a group photo. OK?"

The reporter pulled out her notebook.

"So how did this come about?" she asked.

"It was all down to these children," Ashani explained. "They help with back-room tasks here every Saturday, and when they heard I needed to raise funds to create a new wing, they decided to organize the Waggy Tails Walk."

"Lots of the kennels need repairs," Jaya said breathlessly.

Harper nodded. "And there was a dog called Bingo who needed a home and there wasn't enough space for him."

"So that's when we decided to do something to help," Daniel added.

"After all, we wouldn't have our pups if it wasn't for Underdogs?" said Arlo.

"You have Underdogs pups?" the reporter asked.

They all nodded proudly.

Ashani smiled. "Lulu, my dog, was originally a rescue. When she arrived at Underdogs we discovered she was pregnant. The children each took one of her puppies."

The reporter's eyes widened. "Are they here?"

Ashani pointed to the pups' play area.

The reporter turned to the photographer. "Let's get a group shot with the puppies."

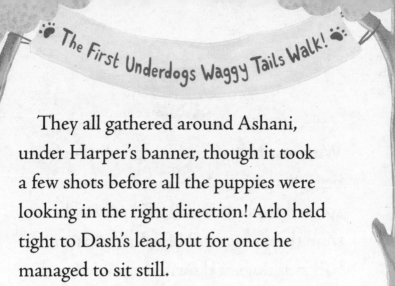

They all gathered around Ashani, under Harper's banner, though it took a few shots before all the puppies were looking in the right direction! Arlo held tight to Dash's lead, but for once he managed to sit still.

"Perfect!" the photographer called.

With just half an hour to go, the entrants began to gather. Arlo and the others spotted loads of friends from school and soon the air was full of woofs, yips and barks, as dogs and owners mingled at the start line. Arlo held tight to Dash's lead as he bounded around, saying hello.

"At least he's not scared, like Bonnie," Jaya said, cuddling her cowering puppy.

Arlo laughed. "This is definitely Dash's idea of heaven!"

Just before two o'clock Ashani's voice blared through the microphone. "Welcome! I'm delighted to see everyone here for the first ever Underdogs Waggy Tails Walk."

Everyone cheered.

"I hope you all have a wonderful afternoon, but before we set off, I'd just

144

like to say a huge thank you to six special people. Jaya, Arlo, Daniel, Harper, Elsa and Willow – aka Puppy Club. Give us a wave!"

The crowd craned their necks to look at them as they all waved. Arlo felt like a celebrity!

"Without them, this walk would not be happening," Ashani continued. "Three cheers for Puppy Club! Hip hip…"

"HOORAY!" the crowd shouted.

After that, everyone gathered under the start sign, as the photographer took another photo. Ashani outlined the rules and reminded everyone to be generous at the refreshments stall as there were cakes for sale baked by a prize-winning baker! Arlo beamed with pride.

Finally, it was time to set off. As they waited on the start line in their group, Arlo turned to the others. "Thanks so much for your support, guys. It's been tough but we made it!"

"We never doubted you for a minute!" said Daniel.

Arlo grinned at his friends. "Puppy Club is the best!"

146

The walk started well, with Arlo and Dash walking along calmly beside everyone else. Suddenly though, a squirrel ran across the path, sending Dash into a frenzy as he tried to pull Arlo after it.

"Dash, no!" said Arlo, panicking as he let Dash lead him along. "Calm down. Dash, hang on! I can't believe you're doing this after all our hard work!"

"Arlo! Remember Jan's advice," Daniel called. "Don't panic, and use your instructions."

Arlo took a deep breath. He knew Daniel was right. "Dash! Stop!" he cried, standing his ground and holding on to the lead with all his might. The squirrel was long gone and after a short while, Dash stopped pulling and returned to Arlo's side.

"Well done!" came a voice from behind him. "You handled that perfectly."

He turned round to see Jan, with her retriever trotting along beside her. She gave him a thumbs up.

He beamed back at her, feeling proud of himself, and of Dash.

After the squirrel incident, to Arlo's relief, Dash mostly walked to heel and as they headed towards the finish sign, he could not have felt prouder. They took the pups straight over to the refreshments stall, which was being looked after by Sue, Arlo's dad and Sophie, to buy some doggy treats.

"You were amazing, Dash!" said Arlo, as his puppy wolfed down the treats.

"He really was," agreed Jaya.

Willow grinned. "Teamwork makes the dream work."

As the stream of entrants finished, many came over to the refreshments stall for a well-earned treat and the Puppy Clubbers took it in turns to look after each other's puppy while they helped out. After half an hour, there was nothing left.

"Every last cake sold!" said Ashani, who'd wandered over with Jan.

"I just wanted to say well done to all of you, but particularly to you, Arlo," Jan said.

Arlo's grin couldn't get any bigger. He bent down and gave Dash a huge hug. "Thank you. I loved every minute. Apart from the squirrel bit! I didn't love that."

Everyone laughed.

"Any cakes left?" came a voice.

Arlo looked up to see Lulu and her little dog Snoops.

"I'm so sorry, we've sold out," said Elsa.

Lulu smiled. "I'm not surprised, with Arlo doing the baking."

Arlo reached under the table for a paper bag and handed it to her. "When you said you'd come, I kept you one of each."

Lulu's face lit up. "Well, for that, have an extra donation!" She handed him a twenty-pound note. "Keep the change!"

Arlo gasped. "Thank you so much!"

"Look out for the article in Monday's

paper!" the reporter called over as she and the photographer waved goodbye.

"Thank you!" Ashani called back. She turned to Arlo and the others. "Most of all, thanks to you six. Once again, your teamwork has amazed me. Those pups are very lucky to have you as owners! Now we'd better get everything cleared up."

"I wish there were some cakes left for us!" said Willow sadly. "They looked so good."

"I might be able to help you there," Sue chipped in. She handed Arlo a large tin. Inside, were a batch of six perfect pup cakes. "Sophie and I made extra during the week. A reward for all your hard work!"

Everyone cheered and Arlo handed the tin round. Down at his feet, Dash barked and nuzzled into his legs. Arlo scooped him up.

"What a journey you two have had," said Dad. "And I don't just mean on the Waggy Tails Walk!"

Arlo nodded, his mind flying back to the *Britain's Best Baker* final on television. Was that really just three weeks ago? Such a lot had happened since then. Not least, he now had a well-trained puppy. Some work to do, yes, but Dash was a dream compared to then. "Thank you, Dash, for everything," he said, rubbing his nose into his puppy's curly head. "Told you, didn't I? We make a great team."

Arlo's Pupcakes Recipe

You will need a grown-up to help you
with this recipe. This will make
24 cupcakes.

Preheat the oven to 180 degrees/ 160
degrees fan or gas mark 4 and fill two
12-hole muffin tins with 24
paper cake cases.

Ingredients

For the muffins:

200g softened butter

200g caster sugar

50g cocoa

175g self-raising flour

4 eggs, beaten

For the chocolate buttercream:
140g softened butter
280g icing sugar
50g cocoa powder
1-2 tablespoons of milk
Quarter teaspoon of vanilla essence
White and milk chocolate buttons and
jelly sweets for the decorations.

Method:
In a large bowl, beat the butter and sugar
together with a wooden spoon until light
and fluffy.

Add in the cocoa powder and flour and
stir thoroughly. Then pour in the beaten
eggs and mix to combine.

Spoon the mixture into the paper cases.
Ask your grown-up to help you put the

muffin tins in the oven. Bake for 15-20 minutes. With help from your grown-up remove the muffin tins from the oven and leave to cool.

To make the chocolate buttercream, beat the butter in a large bowl until soft. Add half of the icing sugar and mix until smooth then stir in the the cocoa powder. Add the remaining icing sugar and one tablespoon of the milk and vanilla essence and beat the mixture until creamy and smooth. Beat in the remaining milk, if necessary, to loosen the mixture.

Spread a layer of buttercream over each pupcake and decorate with sweets to make a puppy face. Enjoy your delicious pupcakes!

Vegan Choc Banana Pupcakes

Bake a delicious vegan pupcake using the ingredients below. Follow the same method as for Arlo's pupcakes, substituting the mashed banana for the eggs. This will make 12 cupcakes.

Ingredients:

100g vegan butter or baking spread

100g caster sugar

100g self-raising flour

25g cocoa powder

1 large ripe mashed banana

For the chocolate buttercream, substitute vegan butter or baking spread for butter and use water instead of milk to soften the mixture. Decorate the top with vegan sweets to make a pup face!

Catherine Jacob loves writing stories for children and also loves dogs, so *Puppy Club* is a dream to write. She lives in Yorkshire with her husband, three young children and a Labradoodle puppy. Many of the *Puppy Club* puppies' escapades are based on real-life events!

Catherine is also passionate about the environment and as a TV reporter, she has travelled around the world, including the Arctic and the Amazon, but she's happiest back at her writing desk, drinking tea and eating biscuits.

Hailing from Hampshire, Rachael Saunders
is an illustrator with a passion for storytelling
and character design. Her distinctive, bright
and joyful work spans the worlds of children's
literature, animation, product design
and handbags.

When she's not creating beautifully whimsical
illustrations, she can be found playing tennis
or getting lost in the New Forest while
walking her dog.

Have you read...

Lulu, a new arrival at Underdogs, is expecting puppies. Could it be the perfect moment for Jaya and her friends to persuade their parents to let them have a dog?

Elsa loves her gorgeous puppy Coco but her family's two cats aren't so welcoming and chase the terrified pup all over the house. Will the three ever be friends?

Look out for the next Puppy Club book coming soon...